The Cake That Wasn't a Cake

Level 11 – Lime

Helpful Hints for Reading at Home

The graphemes (written letters) and phonemes (units of sound) used throughout this series are aligned with Letters and Sounds. This offers a consistent approach to learning whether reading at home or in the classroom.

HERE ARE SOME COMMON WORDS THAT YOUR CHILD MIGHT FIND TRICKY:

water	where	would	know	thought	through	couldn't
laughed	eyes	once	we're	school	can't	our

TOP TIPS FOR HELPING YOUR CHILD TO READ:

- Encourage your child to read aloud as well as silently to themselves.
- Allow your child time to absorb the text and make comments.
- Ask simple questions about the text to assess understanding.
- Encourage your child to clarify the meaning of new vocabulary.

This book focuses on developing independence, fluency and comprehension. It is a lime level 11 book band.

The Cake That Wasn't a Cake

Written by
William Anthony

Illustrated by
Rosie Groom

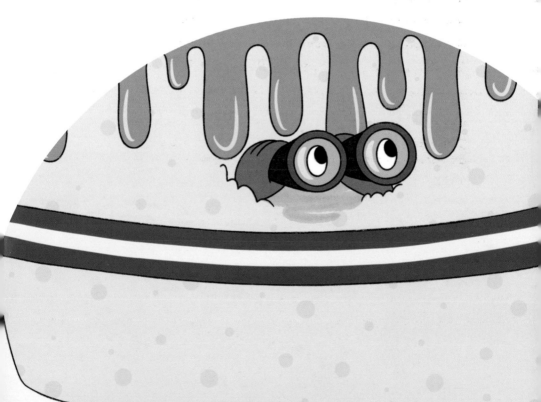

Chapter One

A Story of Two Families

This is a story of two families. They do not like each other at all. In fact, they have been enemies for more than thirty-four years. Yes, you read that right. THIRTY-FOUR.

It's also a story about blueberry pies. Did you know that blueberry pies make excellent weapons in a battle? Don't worry – most people don't know that.

There's a lot of revenge too. Battle plans as well – there are a few of those. That's never a good sign.

Oh, and cake! It's a story about that. Well, kind of. This is a story about a cake that wasn't a cake.

Chapter Two

Birthday Surprise

The party poppers went beside the party hats. The napkins went beside the party poppers. The paper plates went beside the napkins and the party bags went beside the paper plates.

No, wait, that wasn't going to work. Where was the huge, enormous, mega-sized mountain of a cake going to go? No, this wasn't right.

Of course, Tim didn't have a cake yet, but he was sure one was on its way.

He placed the napkins on the paper plates, put the party bags on the napkins, stacked the party poppers on the party bags and topped it off with the party hats.

The leaning tower of pieces was great until it leaned a bit too far. Oh well, it was just extra room for cake.

10:06 PM. Tim needed sleep. The party preparation had gobbled up all of his energy. "Night, Mum. Night, Nanna," he tooted as he dragged his feet up the stairs.

"Night, Tim," they chirped back. They waited until Tim's door clinked shut. Then the smiles fell off their faces.

"What are we going to do?" worried Tim's nanna.

"I don't know," replied Tim's mum. "He's been talking all week about a huge cake, but we just don't have the money for one."

"Well we can't give him a cupcake!" said Nanna. "I'll ask Maureen for a favour in the morning and see if she can make us one."

The moon shone through the window as Tim sat up in his bed. His mouth was dry. He came down the stairs, through the hall, past the wonky photos and into the kitchen. A glass of water would do the trick. He walked into the dining room and was more awake than ever.

On the table stood a huge, enormous, mega-sized mountain of a cake. Tim's jaw hit the carpet.

He got up close, drooling at each layer from top to bottom. Every layer was better than the last, except for the bottom one. The bottom one was weird. A pair of tiny binoculars poked their way through the icing when Tim was looking at that one.

Chapter Three

The Marrones

"ARRGHH!" screeched Tim. "ARRGHH!" squeaked the cake. Tim could hear whispers. He took a nervous step towards the cake, followed by another, followed by the whispers going silent.

"Don't be takin' any more steps, pal," said the cake. Tim froze. "Can I trust ya? No funny business?" it said again. Tim nodded. The binoculars disappeared. "Okay boys, open up. We're good to go."

The cake burst open and lots of little brown mice poured out of the icing door. Each was dressed in a little black suit, with tiny paws peeping out of their trousers and sleeves. They scattered all over the kitchen. The last mouse plodded out of the cake. It was dressed even smarter than the others and walked with pride.

"My name is Marco Marrone," it said. "And you are?"

Tim fainted.

"Come on tough guy, wake up," said Marco. He was perched on Tim's chin. Tim blinked his eyes and sat up. "I've got some explaining to do," admitted Marco.

Marco was head of the Marrone family. The Marrones were a family of Italian mice who lived in New York City, in the United States of America. They had travelled to the UK to settle an old score in London.

"The tale starts in 1984," explained Marco. "My family moved to London from Milano, Italia. At the time, my mother's father's father's mother's brother's mother's father's sister's brother's mother's father's father was the head of the family, and he came to the UK to set up a business selling blueberry pies."

"He fell in love with a mouse.
She was head of the Whites,
a mouse family here in London.
He invited her into
the business, but she got greedy.
She tried to steal the business and
leave us Marrones without a dime.

"Two years later, our families weren't friendly anymore, and the Great Mousey Battle of 1986 began. The Whites won by dunking Don Marrone headfirst into his own blueberry pie.

"We Marrones had to run away. We crossed the ocean and ended up in New York. But now, the time has finally come to return to London and regain our family's honour.

"We had to sneak in undetected inside the cake because... Here's the catch, my friend," said Marco. "The Whites... They live in your garden."

Chapter Four

The Whites

"Oi, Bridget! I'm going to squash you like a grape!" yelled a little mouse as it tried to shout above the chaos and noise.

"QUIET!" boomed a voice from the back. The tunnel went silent. "Pack it in, I'm trying to blow-dry my whiskers."

"Sorry, Stella," the mice said together. There was a knock at the tunnel door.

Stella answered the door to Tim's big face.
She screamed and scuttled out of sight.
"Errr... are you Stella White? Head of the
White family?" bumbled Tim. Stella poked one
eye around the door.
"Who are you?" she blubbered.
"I'm Tim. A weird mouse in a suit asked me to
give you this," Tim replied. He handed Stella
a tiny note, not much bigger than his
fingernail.

We never forget.

Many years ago, your family took our business, our money and our pride. The day has come for us to take it back.

It seems the Whites have lost their touch. We have secretly invaded and you haven't noticed a thing.

We had planned a surprise attack, but Tim had a better idea - one where no whiskers need to be bent and no tails need to be squished.

Tomorrow, Tim will host a meeting between you and I (it's his birthday today, so he's a tad busy). At the meeting, you and the Whites must surrender everything to us.

If you don't, 1986 will repeat itself - but this time, the result will not be the same.

Marco Marrone

Stella gulped. She knew that giant cake wasn't supposed to be walking by itself. "Where's Annie?" she shouted down the tunnel. Annie was Stella's advisor, but she was out on mousey business. "Well, where's Walter then?"

"He's busy cooking," yelled Bridget.

Stella had no choice – she was going to have to face Marco herself.

Chapter Five

The Great Mousey Summit

Tim sat with his legs crossed. There was a tense atmosphere at the bottom of the garden. Marco was sat patiently on a tiny stool.

The grass began to rustle. Two little ears travelled above the greenery until two beady eyes came into view.

"Stella White. We meet at last," Marco said, with a confident shuffle of his bottom. "Marco Marrone," Stella replied, with a confident twitch of her whiskers. "You are so much like your mother's father's father's mother's brother's mother's father's sister's brother's mother's father's father. You look like you've been dunked in a blueberry pie too."

Marco's eyes narrowed with anger.

"Let's all just calm down for a minute," Tim interrupted. "Err... I have called this meeting today to help settle a 34-year family feud... I think. And... err... also to stop my house being destroyed by mice. Marco, please set out your demands."

"Save it, Marrone," Stella blurted out. "I didn't bring a white flag – there's nothing to surrender. The pie business is gone. It died in 1987."

Marco's eyes got wider again. "1987?" he yelped. "You Whites couldn't even last a year after you won the business from us? I know you lot are run on chaos but that's rubbish, even for you."

"So what? You Marrones may be all posh and organised, but look what happened in 1986," Stella sniggered. "Chaos beat organisation. Chaos sunk the Marrones. Chaos won."

Marco's eyes got narrower again. "You listen here, and you listen good, Stella Whi—"

"STOP IT!" yelled Tim.

Something had hit a nerve. Tim's eyes were watery, and his lip was wobbling.

"I get teased every day about my family!" he blubbered. "I can't watch you two compete over which family you come from as well!" With that, Tim walked away, leaving the mice very confused.

Marco's eyes didn't know which way to move anymore. "Look what you did, Stella!" he finally scoffed.

"Me?" she replied.

"Yes, you!" snapped Marco. "And here's another thing: I officially declare battle between the Marrones and the Whites!"

Chapter Six

The Great Mousey Battle of 2020

Light bundled its way through the gap in the curtains. Tim pulled his sheet over his head. Three nights ago, he went downstairs for a glass of water. Now, he was in the middle of two mouse families at battle. These mice could speak, wear suits and bake blueberry pies. Yet somehow, this wasn't the strangest thing to Tim. The strangest thing was that he cared.

Two taps on the plant pot. That was the cue.

12 little paws patted their way into the long grass. Lots of brown mice stood in a line. In front, Marco Marrone took his position. They stood firm, with their chests puffed out. For a moment, all was still.

Slowly, a ring of white mice began to rise from the grass, trapping the Marrones. The Whites had been planning. Stella was last to rise from the grass.

"This is pretty weak, Marco," she bragged. "THIS was your battle plan? To simply present yourself to me?"
"Not quite," he returned. "THIS was." Marco clicked his fingers. An even larger circle of brown mice rose out of the long grass, trapping Stella's carefully placed circle of white mice.

Marco clicked his fingers twice more.
On the first click, the Marrones picked up
blueberries. On the second click, Marco
started the Great Mousey Battle of 2020.

Blueberries flew and squeaking noises filled
the air. Rosa Marrone got Barry White in the
bottom with one blueberry before squashing
one over Janine White's head. Direct hits.

Stefano Marrone preferred sneak attacks.
As Tammy and Greg White fled for cover
in the bush, he tipped a watering can
on them, soaking them wet through.

The Whites were losing, and losing badly.

Her backup plan sat waiting, but it wasn't waiting alone. Sat beside it was Marco Marrone.

"You really thought you would try to dunk me in a blueberry pie?" said Marco, tapping on the pastry. "One thing you should know about me, Stella, is I am not like the Marrones of 1986. I am always one step ahead." Marco clicked his fingers one last time. Maria and Rosa Marrone emerged from behind Stella and grabbed her.

They led her out of the tunnel into the open. Marco followed with the pie.

"Attention, White family members!" boomed Marco. "This battle is over!" He signalled to Rosa and Maria, who picked up Stella by the feet. "I'm sorry, Stella. I am. But this is for my mother's father's father's mother's brother's mother's father's sister's brother's mother's father's father."

On his cue, Rosa and Maria began to lower Stella headfirst towards the blueberry pie...

Chapter Seven

Tim's Troubles

"STOP RIGHT NOW, MARCO!"

Tim stood tall, stopping the dunking from going any further. He had seen the battle from his room after a wayward blueberry had hit his window.

"I can't watch this go on any longer," he said.

"Every day that I go to school, people tease me about the family I come from. I tried to help you because you were teasing each other about the families you come from as well! No one deserves that," Tim explained. "You might be from different families, but you're all mice. You should be looking out for each other, not battling!"

Tim could do no more. It was up to Marco and Stella now – battle forever or put their problems behind them...

Chapter Eight

The Great Mousey-Human Battle of 2020

Tim was sat on the school field reading a book. He never did find out how the Great Mousey Battle of 2020 ended. He made his point and left it up to the mice. Stella White could very well be blue right now.

Two shadows crept up on Tim.

"Did you get a giant cake for your birthday?" said the boy.

"I did!" chuckled the girl. "What about you?" she asked the boy back.

"I did too! But I heard Tim got a measly little cupcake for his..." the boy joked.

Tim wasn't going to take the teasing anymore. He stood up tall.

"Go away or I'll make you!" he warned them.

"Oh yeah?" said the boy. "You and what army?"

"This one," said a little voice. Marco Marrone stepped out from behind Tim's leg.

"Oh, and this one," said another little voice. Stella White stepped out from behind Tim's other leg.

The two mice looked across to each other and winked. They both raised a paw and on the click of their fingers, they started the Great Mousey-Human Battle of 2020.

All the Marrones and all the Whites jumped out of bushes and popped up through the grass and unleashed havoc. Barry and Walter White used blueberry slingshots, while Maria, Rosa and Stefano Marrone dropped blueberry pies on the boy and girl from the tree.

The boy and the girl ran for cover, but they were already blue from head to toe.

The mice all squeaked in victory! Stella and Marco fist bumped, pleased that their plan had worked.

Tim wasn't quite sure he'd seen what he'd just seen. He had just watched more mice than he could count – some dressed in suits, others dressed in t-shirts – jump out from the grass and bushes at his school and launch an attack on two mean children, using blueberries as weapons. He blinked a few times. No, it wasn't a dream. Mice really were stood in front of him with big grins on their faces.

"But... how... wha... where... di..." bumbled Tim. He couldn't make a full sentence.

"Right," said Marco, dusting himself off. "Anyone want cake?"

Chapter Nine

A Story of One Family

This was a story of one family. The Marrones and the Whites had gone from being enemies to a big family that worked brilliantly together.

Marco and Stella were no longer trying to battle each other. With Tim's help, they realised they weren't so different after all. In fact, it turned out that they were a good team.

Marco and the Marrones moved back to New York, while Stella and the Whites settled back into London life. They visited each other often and had even talked about opening a blueberry pie shop together. Where have we heard that one before?

As for Tim, his mum and his nanna, they were tucking into a gift that Marco had left as a thank you.

The Cake That Wasn't a Cake

1) When did the first Great Mousey Battle take place?

    a) 2020

    b) 1984

    c) 1986

2) How did the Whites win the first Great Mousey Battle?

3) Why does Tim want to help the Marrones and the Whites?

4) How did Marco and Stella solve their differences? Who helped them?

5) How did Tim feel after the Great Mousey–Human Battle of 2020? Have you ever felt this way? When?

©2021 **BookLife Publishing Ltd.**
King's Lynn, Norfolk PE30 4LS

ISBN 978-1-83927-411-4

The Cake That Wasn't A Cake
Written by William Anthony
Illustrated by Rosie Groom

An Introduction to BookLife Readers...

Our Readers have been specifically created in line with the London Institute of Education's approach to book banding and are phonetically decodable and ordered to support each phase of Letters and Sounds.

Each book has been created to provide the best possible reading and learning experience. Our aim is to share our love of books with children, providing both emerging readers and prolific page-turners with beautiful books that are guaranteed to provoke interest and learning, regardless of ability.

BOOK BAND GRADED using the Institute of Education's approach to levelling.

PHONETICALLY DECODABLE supporting each phase of Letters and Sounds.

EXERCISES AND QUESTIONS to offer reinforcement and to ascertain comprehension.

BEAUTIFULLY ILLUSTRATED to inspire and provoke engagement, providing a variety of styles for the reader to enjoy whilst reading through the series.

AUTHOR INSIGHT:
WILLIAM ANTHONY

Despite his young age, William Anthony's involvement with children's education is quite extensive. He has written over 60 titles with BookLife Publishing so far, across a wide range of subjects. William graduated from Cardiff University with a 1st Class BA (Hons) in Journalism, Media and Culture, creating an app and a TV series, among other things, during his time there.

William Anthony has also produced work for the Prince's Trust, a charity created by HRH The Prince of Wales, that helps young people with their professional future. He has created animated videos for a children's education company that works closely with the charity.

This book focuses on developing independence, fluency and comprehension. It is a lime level 11 book band.

47